Wendy & Black

The Mystery House

Amma Lee

INTRODUCTION

Wendy Michaels is a fifteen-year-old high school girl with the ability to speak with cats, a power which women from Wendy's family acquire every one hundred years. Wendy always enjoyed helping people, which is why Wendy and her pet cat, Black, decided to become detectives. When an alleged haunted and abandoned house down the street from Wendy and Black is bought by someone, Wendy needs to investigate the house and the buyer. Even though Black believes that the investigation is pointless, he goes along with it. But what Wendy and Black didn't know was that their investigation was about to take a paranormal turn.

CHAPTER ONE

"Wendy!" Black called out as he searched throughout the house for Wendy. Normally she was home from school by then, so he didn't understand why she wasn't responding to him. "Her book bag is here," Black said as he noticed that her pink and black book bag was by the kitchen door.

"Hi, Black." Black's head whipped around when he heard a voice similar to Wendy's, but he sighed when he saw that it was just Mrs. Michaels, Wendy's mother. She quickly stooped down, and he tried his best to get out of her reach as she started to pick him up, but he was unsuccessful.

"Put me down." Black said, but he knew that she wasn't going to be able to understand him. In the Michaels family, every century a female was granted the ability to speak to cats. Wendy had gained the ability to talk to cats when she was four years old, and she loved it!

"You must be looking for Wendy. The two of you are

inseparable!" She said as she cradled Black in her arms like a baby. He wasn't fond of it when Wendy did it, and he wasn't fond of it when Mrs. Michaels did it either.

"I am, so can you put me down?" Unable to understand the brooding cat, Mrs. Michaels decided to hold him in her arms for a few more moments before placing him down.

"Wendy will be back in a few minutes; I sent her on an errand." Black nodded his head. He wasn't able to communicate with other people, other than Wendy, verbally, but he could still give people visual clues of what he wanted or his response to something.

"Fine," Black said, walking into the living room. He jumped onto the couch and stretched out. Black yawned loudly and decided to wait till Wendy walked through the door. He found himself to be incredibly bored, and he knew that Wendy would have many stories to tell him.

At fifteen years of age, Wendy always came home and told Black about everything that went on at her school that day. She was always very animated about it. He was so accustomed to her tales that it wasn't a wonder as to why he was feeling antsy for her to come back home.

"I hope she doesn't take too long." Black wasn't exactly always the gentlest cat, especially when he was bored, but he was willing to wait till Wendy came home in exchange for an interesting story. He was pretty sure that whatever her mother had her doing wouldn't take her the rest of the day to do it. Plus, she was a young girl, and he knew that Mrs. Michaels wouldn't want her out by herself at a particular time at night.

"She should have just come and got me when she came home." Black was a little surprised that she came home and didn't say anything to him even though she had to go right back out of the house. Normally she would have at least said hello to him when she first arrived home from school. Maybe something serious had happened that made Mrs. Michaels send her back out as soon as she had stepped foot into the door.

"Black!" the high pitch voice that he had grown to love resounded throughout the small living room and Black jumped off of the couch. Wendy walked in the house with a large brown bag in her hand and Black eyed it for a moment before he said anything.

"What took you so long? I've been incredibly bored." He said and shook out his black fur. Wendy placed the bag on the floor and for the second time that day, Black was being cradled in someone's arms like a baby.

"I'm sorry, did you miss me?" she asked as she rubbed her face in his soft fur. Sighing, Black nodded his head.

"I suppose that I've missed you. Well, I've missed your stories at least." Wendy pouted and sat Black on the floor.

"So you only missed me because you were bored then?" she asked Black, but she already knew the answer. She knew that Black cared deeply for her, but he wasn't a cat that liked to show affection too much.

"Well..." Black paused and thought about how he wanted to answer Wendy's question. He enjoyed teasing Wendy, but he suspected that he might have offended her by saying that he only missed her because of her stories. "I did miss listening to you tell me about your adventures at school; however, that's not the only thing that I missed." He mumbled that last part. Wendy was the world to him, but being sentimental wasn't his forte.

"What else did you miss then?" Wendy asked, and a grin spread across her face. Black turned his furry little head away from her at that moment.

".... you." Black said, and Wendy squealed. Picking him up quickly again, Wendy planted kisses all over his grumpy little face. "Come on now! You're messing up my fur!" he protested, but she continued to kiss him.

"I missed you too!" she cooed, and Black sighed. He knew that there was no point in struggling in Wendy's arms. Black allowed Wendy to kiss him, and he couldn't help but smile. I love this girl, he thought and looked up when Mrs. Michaels walked back into the living room.

"Where's the bag that Mrs. Stevens should have given you?" Wendy's mother asked and Wendy placed Black back down onto the floor. He shook his fur similar to how a dog would have done and sat down on the floor.

"It's right here." Wendy said and picked up the brown bag. "What's in it?" Wendy asked curiously as her mother looked in the bag.

"A welcome kit for the new neighbor that moved into that house down the street." Wendy's eyebrows went up in surprise.

"You mean the haunted house?!" Wendy couldn't believe that someone had bought that house. Mrs. Michaels laughed at her daughter's outburst.

"Sweetheart, you're fifteen years old. Do you still believe in that stuff?" Wendy's mother asked and laughed. Wendy blushed, but folded her arms.

"There's been a lot of mysteries involving that house. Who's to say that that house isn't haunted just because we've personally not seen anything?" Wendy asked, and her mother just smiled.

"Okay, Wendy if that's what you want to believe." Mrs. Michaels thought that it was healthy for a child to have imagination, so she didn't say anything more about the matter. Besides, it wasn't as if she was hurting anyone by not telling Wendy not to believe in things like that. "I'll get a few more items out of the kitchen." She said and walked into the kitchen.

"I'm with your mother on this one." Black said and

walked over to Wendy. "Don't let what those other humans say frighten you." Wendy looked at Black and placed her hands on her hips.

"It is true Black, that house is creepy. Janet and Timothy told me that they hear strange noises coming from the house whenever they walk past it." Black sighed, and his eyes glittered as he stared at her.

"Janet and Timothy thought they heard something." Black said while looking into Wendy's eyes. "And from everything that you have told me about those two, I don't consider them to be reliable sources." It was true that Janet and Timothy exaggerated some things that they told Wendy, but she didn't consider them to be liars.

"Alright, the best way to find out something is to dig deeper, right?" Wendy asked, and a small smile lit up her face.

"Yeah." Black said hesitantly. Black knew exactly where Wendy was trying to go with this conversation, and he didn't want any part of it.

"Well, let's go and check it out." Black sighed irritably.

"Wendy, there's nothing to investigate. The house is just a bit run down that's all. Plus, someone lives there!" Black exclaimed. "We'd be evading the human's privacy if we were to stake out his house in attempts to solve a case not worth investigating."

Wendy didn't agree with what Black was saying. Everyone thought that the house down the street was out of the ordinary and Wendy couldn't help but to think that something might be going on with the man who had moved into the house.

"I'll buy you a toy mouse." Black's ears perked up at what Wendy said, and she smiled in victory. Black might have been a cool cat, but he adored playing with his toys. Black grumbled for a few moments and then hung his head low in defeat.

"I don't know what exactly it is that you're trying to accomplish, but count me in." He hated that he allowed Wendy to persuade him into investigating an alleged haunted house. He knew nothing good would come out of it, but since he was going to get a new toy out of the deal, he'd let Wendy have her fun.

"Great! Let's walk down the street and see what we can see." Wendy said and headed towards the door and opened it. Black sighed one last time as he reluctantly followed her.

CHAPTER TWO

"Didn't mom say that somebody is staying here?" Wendy asked when they made it to the rundown house on the corner of their street.

"Yes, but it doesn't look inhabitable." Black said. He did find it odd that someone was living in a place so horrid looking. "Are you sure that this is the right house?" Black asked then. Wendy didn't normally walk down this side of the street, so he hadn't seen the house for himself. Looking at the house now, he could understand why people might have thought that the house was "creepy." It did have a somewhat spooky vibe to it.

"Of course this is the right house." Wendy's high voice said quickly. Even though it was still light outside, she wasn't able to see anything in the room even though the blinds were open. "I think someone must have lied to my mom, the door is all boarded up, so there's no way that someone's living here." Wendy scratched her head and looked at the house in confusion. She wondered who had told her mother and their neighbor that someone was living in this house now.

"Hmmm… I don't sense anybody in the house." Black said as he closed his eyes and listened. Wendy looked at Black, then at the house before she closed her eyes as well. She knew that she wouldn't be able to hear things that Black could since he was a cat and his hearing was more advanced than hers, but she figured that if she focused her ears hard enough she'd be able to hear something as well.

"Well?" Wendy asked when Black opened his eyes again.

"Nothing, I don't hear anything inside." Black shook his head then. What was he doing? Why was he so concerned about not being able to sense anything in the house? If anything, he had just proved that the house wasn't haunted. No, Black knew what was bothering him. The fact that someone was supposedly living in this house and Black wasn't able to sense them was the problem.

"What are you thinking?" Wendy asked as she watched Black stare at the house in deep concentration. He wasn't sure about what to make of their current situation, and he didn't want to discuss it with Wendy since there wasn't much to tell her.

"I can hear your mother calling us." Black said, and Wendy's eyes widened. Even though they were on the same street, they were a couple of blocks away from their home.

"Seriously?" Wendy asked, surprised. "Well if you're able to hear her from where we're at she must need me back at the house." Black nodded his head and followed behind Wendy as she walked down the street. He hadn't really heard Wendy's mother calling her. He had only wanted to get away from that house. He didn't know what to think about the house at that moment, but he did feel a sense of unease when he was near it.

"Yes, mom?" Wendy asked as soon as she and Black walked into the house. Her mother looked up at her and raised an eyebrow.

"Yes, what?" was her mother's response.

"Didn't you call me? Black said he heard you calling my name." Wendy looked at Black, and he had his same somber expression plastered on his face. Her mother shook her head.

"No, I didn't call you." Her mother said and turned towards the TV again. Wendy started making her way to her room.

"You're getting old Black." She teased Black as she closed her bedroom door. "Your ears must be playing tricks on you." Wendy laughed, and Black jumped onto her bed and laid down.

"You might be right about that." Normally he would

have gotten defensive, but he allowed Wendy to have her fun because he didn't want to tell her that he had lied when he told her that her mother had called her.

"Maybe we just need to clean them out." Wendy said as she sat down and turned on the computer. Black allowed a loud hiss to escape between his teeth, and Wendy couldn't help but to laugh. Black hated to have the inside of his ears cleaned, and he always struggled when she tried to do it.

"Keep that swab away from my ears!" he hissed again, and Wendy laughed. Black was so adorable when he was mad, so she decided to tease him a little bit more.

"You can either take that or a bath, so which one will it be?" Black groaned. He hated both, but if he had to choose one that was more tolerable than the other, he'd have to go with getting his ears cleaned. Instead of answering her though Black decided to change the subject.

"What are you looking up?" Black asked when he noticed that Wendy was typing in something in the Google search bar.

"I'm Googling that house. I want to see if anything weird has ever happened inside of it." Black decided that he wanted to clear his head some before he thought about that house down the street again. At first Black found Wendy's notions of the house being haunted to be completely absurd, and he still felt that way actually, but he would be lying if he said that there wasn't anything odd about the house.

"I'm going to rest for a little while so keep it down." Black told Wendy as he closed his eyes. Wendy whispered okay to him and after a while Black could no longer hear the soft typing of Wendy's fingers on the keyboard as he drifted off to sleep.

When Black woke up, he was surprised to see that it was morning, and Wendy had already left for school.

"I didn't think that I'd sleep that long." Black said as he stretched and leaped off of the bed. Looking at the clock that was on Wendy's nightstand, he saw that it was 8:30. He knew that Wendy was definitely at school at that moment. When Black walked in the kitchen, he heard no movement in the house, so he concluded that everyone had left for the day.

"Good," he said and went straight for his bowl of food. He was looking forward to alone time today because it would give him enough time to think and he wouldn't be able to do that when Mrs. Michaels was there. It wasn't like Black thought that she was a bad person or anything like that, but he did think that she was a little too grabby.

"I see where Wendy gets her loving ways from." Black said as he finished his bowl of food. Black drank some of his water and went back into the bedroom to see what notes Wendy had written down about the house down the street. Wendy and Black had been detectives for a little more than two years now, and they had solved many cases together. Wendy didn't have a detective eye like Black did, but she gave it all that she could to help Black.

Jumping on Wendy's chair and then onto her computer desk, Black read the notes that she had scribbled down about the house.

****

"Wendy!" Wendy turned around when she heard somebody call out her name.

"Hi Janet, I haven't seen you all day." Wendy said and hugged her friend. Janet was one of her best friends at Crystal High school. Her other best friend was Keith Johnson, but he had been out sick for the past week with a cold.

"I just got here, but hey did you hear?" Wendy had nodded her head before Janet continued. She knew what her friend wanted to tell her, so Wendy decided to beat her to the punch.

"About someone moving into that haunted house?" Janet nodded her head and leaned in closer to Wendy.

"Isn't that crazy, who'd honestly want to live there?" Wendy took her chemistry book out of her locker and made her way towards her classroom with Janet walking beside her.

"I went to look at the house yesterday to see if it's true, but it looked the same way as it normally does." Janet shook her head then.

"Timothy saw an old man leaving the house this morning when he was walking here." Wendy's eyes widened at that. She thought about how Black had said he couldn't sense a presence in the house. Was it possible that they had just missed the man?

"But the house is boarded up still." Wendy said in astonishment, and Janet shrugged her arms.

"Timothy said that the man looked creepy, so he probably likes the way the house looks." Wendy's curly hair shook as she shivered. She had done some research on Google the night before regarding the house, but she hadn't found anything bad that had happened in the house. Wendy had come across a forum with hundreds of other people saying how creepy the house was though.

"I should talk to Black about this." Wendy said as Janet rambled on and on about how something must be wrong with the old man.

"What did you say?" Janet asked Wendy, and she shook her head.

"Oh, nothing." She said and smiled. "What else did Timothy tell you?" Janet walked into Wendy's class with her and told her everything that Timothy had told her before Wendy's chemistry teacher walked into the class.

"I'll tell you the rest later." Janet said as she hurried out of the classroom so that she could go to her own. Wendy took out her notebook and wrote down everything that Janet had told her in the hopes that Black would be able to figure something out with the information that she had acquired.

****

When classes ended for the day, she decided that she'd take the long way home. She wanted to see if anything new had occurred with the house down the street. When Janet offered to walk home with her, Wendy told her a quick lie and said that she was going to go to Keith's house to give him notes and homework assignments from their Algebra class.

Let's walk home tomorrow." Wendy said, and Janet nodded her head. Black had told Wendy a while ago never to let anybody know that she was investigating something. People had eyes and ears everywhere, and if the wrong person found out she was a detective, something bad might happen.

"Okay, see you later Wendy." Janet said, and she made her way towards the direction of Timothy's locker. Wendy exhaled in relief and grabbed her things out of her locker. As she made her way towards the exit, she thought of Black. Wendy knew that Black would be angry with her for going to the house without him, but she wasn't going to try and break in it or anything like that. She just wanted to see if something was different about the house and if there were any signs of somebody living there yet.

"Bye Wendy!" Wendy turned at the sound of one of her friend's voices and she waved at the person who had spoken to her. Wendy was a very popular girl because she was kind to everyone. Many people viewed her as a lovely girl because of her helpful ways. Wendy's desire to help people and investigate things that might harm someone was the main reason why she wanted to be a detective.

"Bye!" she waved and picked up her pace. She normally talked to a few of her friends after school, but today wasn't the day for that. She needed to get to that house as soon as possible before she missed something important. "Don't lose your focus, Wendy." Wendy said to herself as she made it onto the street. When she made it to the house, she was surprised to see Black across the street from the house staring at it intently.

CHAPTER THREE

"Black!" Wendy called out, walking up to Black. Black's head stayed in the direction of the house, but he let one of his glowing eyes roam over to Wendy.

"I thought so." Black said, and Wendy stopped and placed her hands on her hips.

"What do you mean 'I thought so'?" Wendy was angry that Black had gone out of the house without her to investigate the haunted house by himself.

"I thought that you'd come here today without coming to get me first." He said, and Wendy's cheeks turned rosy. It wasn't like she was trying to deceive Black or anything, she had just wanted to get a little bit more information on the place. Black was always so productive when it came to investigating things, and since this case was Wendy's idea, she wanted to be productive as well.

"It's not like I was trying to hide anything from you."

Wendy mumbled and looked away from Black's suspicious glance, but then a frown spread across Wendy's lovely face. "But what are you doing here?" Black was quick to tell Wendy that she was wrong because she was sneaking around, but wasn't he doing the same thing?

"There is something about this house that I don't like." Black said as his eyes went back to the broken down and ruined house. "I've been standing here for two hours, and I feel absolutely no human presence here. I don't even sense that your mom was ever here." Wendy's eyes widened, and she moved in closer to Black.

"My mother was here? When?" she asked. She didn't like the house, and she hated that her mother had gone there after Wendy told her that the house was dangerous.

"She came home a few hours ago and took that bag to the human who is supposed to live here, and she hasn't come back yet and I don't sense her having been here." Wendy's eyes widened in fear.

"Do you think something is wrong? Do you think something has happened to my mother?" Wendy picked up Black then and held him in her arms and hugged him. For Black to say that he felt something off about something always meant that something was wrong. Black would have normally squirmed and tried to get away from Wendy, but he didn't this time. He understood how she felt and knew that the girl was worried about her mother.

"I can't say for sure, I could smell your mom a few feet from here, but the closer I came to the house the less I could smell her. This house is messing up my senses for some reason." Black said and looked at the house. "I don't believe this place is spooky, but there is something paranormal about it." Wendy began breathing hard as fear took over her body.

"We have to find a way in!" Wendy shouted. "There's a possibility that my mother is in there." Black nodded his head in agreement. Wendy's mom's scent ended a few feet from the house and this house was the only thing he couldn't feel anything from, so there was a possibility that Mrs. Michaels was still in the house.

"Come on!" Black said and he jumped out of Wendy's arms. Wendy nodded her head and ran behind Black. It was still light outside so they had to make sure that nobody was watching them. When they were sure that the cost was clear, Wendy and Black walked up the steps and peered into a window.

"Can you see anything?" Wendy asked and Black scanned each area of the room that he could see.

"That's strange." Black said and Wendy looked at the side of his face. Black's dark fur blew softly in the wind.

"What's strange? Please don't keep things like this to yourself." Wendy pleaded with Black.

"There's an odd glowing light in the house." Black said and Wendy quickly turned back to the window and pressed her head into it.

"There is a light!" Wendy exclaimed and Black shushed her.

"If someone is in the house we shouldn't alert them to our presence." Black hissed and Wendy blushed. Black was right, she needed to compose herself because overreacting to every little thing that she saw wasn't going to do them any good.

"Why is the light…? Purple?" Looking at the dim purple light was unsettling to her because she had never seen anybody with that color of light before.

"I don't know, but somebody has to be here for that light to be on." Black said. Black wasn't a human, but he understood simple human mechanics. He knew for a light to be on that there had to be electricity in the house. He also knew that if there was electricity in the house then someone surely had to be paying the electric bill. "I still don't sense a presence, though." Black said, confused. Why was it that he was unable to detect anyone when someone had to have been there?

"The coast is clear." Wendy said, as she went towards the front door and inspected the boards.

"There's no way someone was able to open this door with this board nailed on this tight." Wendy said as she tried to force the board away from the door without any luck.

"Try pulling the board upwards instead of out." Wendy obeyed and the board still wouldn't budge. "Hmmm... there must be another way into the house." Black moved away from the window and looked high and low for an opening until he found a broken window near the stairs.

"Here's a way in." Black said and Wendy made her way over to him. It'll be a tight fit, but Black knew that Wendy would be able to squeeze in.
"This does feel kind of wrong, though, but if my mom's hurt in here then we have no choice but to investigate the house." Wendy picked up some wood that was lying on the ground and knocked away the loose pieces of glass shards.

"Be careful." Black said once Wendy began lowering herself into the dark basement of the house.

"Made it!" Wendy said once her feet touched the floor. Despite the fact that it was hot outside, the basement was cold and damp. "Yuck." Wendy groaned when her hand brushed against the
wet and slimy wall.

"I'm coming in!" Black said and Wendy was barely able to make out his dark fur as he leaped through the window. "This place doesn't feel right." Black said and shivered when his paws sunk into the flooded floor. He hated taking a bath so it was no surprise that he hated the murky water from the basement's floor getting onto his paws.

"Do you want me to pick you up?" Wendy asked. She did feel bad that Black had to endure the water on the ground, but she was also afraid. She had never gone into an abandoned house before, not to mention an allegedly haunted abandoned house. Black shook his head and then shook his fur.

"No, no I can continue like this." Wendy pulled out her cell phone then and lit up the darkened space in front of them. Cobwebs littered the ceiling and debris was all over the floor. "Stay close." Black whispered and looked around. As they walked, they heard water dripping from broken pipes and smelled the sewage from the house's backed up drains.

"My mom probably isn't in here." Wendy said as they walked forward. The sounds the house made as it settled scared her more than anything had ever scared her in her life. "She's probably at home wondering what's taking me so long." Wendy said and Black turned around and looked at her.

"I don't think so Wendy." There's something about the atmosphere here that makes me think she's here even though I cannot sense her." Wendy whimpered. She was terrified, but if Black really thought that her mother was here, Wendy wouldn't forgive herself if she abandoned her mother.

"Okay, but let's find our way upstairs." Wendy said and walked closer to Black. Even though Black was just a cat, Black being around her offered her some comfort. For some odd reason, she figured if anything bad happened, he'd be able to protect her. Almost as if he sensed her thoughts Black turned to look at Wendy again.

"I won't let anything happen to you, Wendy." Wendy blushed and nodded her head. This was why they were best friends, because she knew that no matter what they'd never let each other down. "Stop!" Black said suddenly and Wendy stopped in her tracks.

"What's wrong?" Wendy asked as she fought down the urge to cry.

"Do you hear that?" Black whispered and perked his ears up. He had heard someone, or something, moving above them. "There's something upstairs." Black whispered and Wendy gasped. Her breaths came out fast and rugged so she held her breath so that she could hear what Black was listening out for.

"That is definitely somebody walking upstairs." Wendy wanted to hurry up and get out of the house as soon as possible. "What happens if it's a... g...ghost?" Black rolled his eyes.

"There are two things wrong with what you said." Black began. "First, ghosts do not have a physical form. Therefore, we wouldn't be able to hear them walk."

Black turned around and looked at Wendy. "Second there are no such things as ghosts!" Black wasn't trying to raise his voice to Wendy because he knew that she was afraid, but no matter how strange the house was, Black refused to believe it was because of ghosts.

"Then why can't you sense any people here then?" Wendy asked and walked quicker once Black started moving again.

"I don't know, but problems like this always happen when you're investigating something." Black said. Black believed that all cases would have some type of problem. If they didn't, Black wouldn't view it as a real case. "There's the stairs!" Black shouted once they came across the stairs.

"Are we really going to go up there?" Wendy asked. Even though investigating this house was her idea, she was starting to have a change of heart.

"If your mother is in here we have to help her." Wendy took in a deep breath and nodded her head.

"You're right. I can do this." Wendy said, trying to build up her confidence. The two of them sauntered up the stairs and the sounds that the creaking stairs made unnerved Black as well.

"We're making too much noise. We need to try to walk softer." Wendy started walking up the stairs even slower and on her tiptoes. When they made it to the top of the stairs, they stopped. "You need to see if the door is open." Black said and Wendy sighed. She knew that she was going to have to be the one to open the door because it wasn't like Black could do it.

"It's times like these that I wished you were a person, Black." Wendy said and Black chuckled.

"Its times like these that I'm glad that I'm a cat." Wendy stuck her tongue out at Black when he said this. Wendy did feel a rush of relief wash over her though because she was happy that Black had tried to lighten up the situation.

"Here goes nothing." She said and placed her hand on the cold and wet door knob. When Wendy turned the knob, she was surprised to find that it was open. "I can't believe it's open." She whispered and poked her head out of the door.

"What do you see?" Black asked and moved so that he could look as well.

"The whole room is purple." Wendy whispered and stared at the room wide-eyed. Black looked around the room as well then.

"It's furnished." Black said as he looked at the furniture that was throughout the room. The furniture was covered with a sheet. "That's odd, how come we weren't able to see this from the outside?" he asked himself. Wendy walked over to a covered couch and began lifting up the sheet, but shrieked when a loud crash sounded in the other room.

"Black!" she called out and placed her hand on her chest. She wanted to run, but she didn't know where the exit was. Black was just as startled and ran to the other side of the room and looked on towards the direction of the crash.

"Don't yell." Black said once he had composed himself. If there was someone in the house, they wouldn't be surprised by a cat's cries like they would with a young girl's scream. Wendy's hands shot up and covered her mouth.

"Sorry." She said sheepishly and Black nodded his head. Black came out of the corner and walked over to Wendy. She was trembling in fear and Black wanted to give her some form of comfort so he rubbed his head on her exposed ankles. "I'm alright now." She said and lowered her hand away from her chest.

"We have to check on that Wendy." Black said and Wendy nodded her head. "I'll go first." Black suggested and Wendy gave him a half smile. Since she was the only one who could hear Black talking, if he saw something out of the ordinary Black could alert her without giving her position away.

"Thanks, Black." Wendy said and Black nodded his head. He didn't like the idea one bit, but the odds of him getting hurt were less than the odds of Wendy getting hurt. Black made his way to the partially opened door and pushed his head through it and looked around. "See anything?" Wendy whispered from a distance away.

"Not really." Black said and stepped through the door a little more. The room was so dark that even Black's eyes had a hard time adjusting to it. Maybe he was getting old, Black thought to himself. "Wait right here." He said and stepped all the way through the door. At the end of the room, he saw a small light shining from a crack from under a door, but as he moved across the room, the ground began to shake.

"Black is everything alright?" Wendy asked and stuck her head through the door. Since the room was pitch black and Black's fur was black, she wasn't able to see where he was.

"Woah!" she heard Black shout and she could hear the ground creaking.

"Black, I think the ground is caving in!" Wendy cried out to Black.

"I know!" Black responded. Wendy wanted to run in and find Black before the floor crumbled, but she knew that her added weight would only make the ground cave in faster.

"Black!" Wendy shouted just as the floor boards creaked one last time and then fell to the ground below."

CHAPTER FOUR

"Black!" Wendy called out again. She started to panic a little when Black didn't respond back to her. "Are you alright, Black?" Wendy hated that she wasn't able to see anything. If she could find a light switch, she'd be able to see exactly where the floor caved in at so that she could avoid that area. "I'll help you, Black!" Wendy called out again. Her fingers trembled as she fumbled against the wall for a light switch.

"It has to be somewhere around here." Since there was some light in the house, she knew that the electricity was on. She moved her hand up and down the wall until she found the light switch. "Yes!" she said and turned the lights on and she wasn't surprised to see the room turn a purple color. She looked around the room and noticed just about half of the middle of the room had collapsed.

"This is not good." Wendy said as she made baby steps inside of the room. The room was definitely unstable and she didn't want to risk falling as well. She looked around the room and saw construction tape throughout the entire room with paint and wood on the floor. She saw a ladder and a few chairs pushed along the wall.

"What's going on here?" Wendy asked herself. From the looks of the room, it appeared as if someone was trying to fix it up. She shook her head and stared straight ahead. This wasn't the time to be worrying about things like this. What she needed to focus on was the fact that her best friend had just fallen into a hole.

"Black!" Wendy called out again as she made it to the hole. When she peered into the hole, she wasn't surprised to see that she couldn't see anything.

"Ugh, I'm alright." Came Black's feeble voice. Normally Black's cat ability would have come into play while he was falling, but this time it didn't. Black had fallen down hard onto his back which had knocked the wind out of him. That was why he had been unable to respond to Wendy the first few times she had called out to him.

"Oh thank goodness!" Wendy said as she sunk down to her knees. She didn't know what she would have done if something had happened to Black. "Do you see a way back up?" Wendy asked. She wanted Black to be near her as soon as possible so that she could take him into her arms.

"Yeah I see a way." Black said as he shook out his fur. He had fallen back down into the basement and he was irritated that his fur had gotten damp and dusty. He felt so dirty at that moment that he wasn't willing to lick himself clean. "I guess I'm going to need a bath when we get back home." Black said and Wendy couldn't stifle her laugh. Black knew exactly what to say to keep her mind off of a negative situation.

"You bet you're going to get a bath." Wendy said still grinning. "There's no way that I'm going to let you sleep in my bed like that." Black groaned as he made his way up some of the floorboards that were still intact. Once he had gotten upstairs, Wendy picked him up and placed affectionate kisses on his dusty cheeks.

"Come on now," Black said and chuckled. "I'm alright now." Wendy didn't care if Black smelled horrible from the murky water that he had landed in. Wendy didn't care that she was kissing Black's dirty fur. The only thing that she cared about was the fact that Black was alright and back with her.

"I was so scared." Wendy said and sniffled. Black was very special to her and she couldn't imagine that there'd be a time when he wasn't with her anymore. Black purred and rubbed his cheek against Wendy's mouth. Black wasn't normally this affectionate with Wendy because it was against his nature, but he understood how she felt. Black loved Wendy more than anything in the world.

"I know, I was too." Black said honestly. When he had fallen into that hole, the very first thing that he thought about was Wendy. He knew if he wasn't able to get back up that Wendy would be alone in that place and he couldn't bear the thought of that. He knew that the house was dangerous, not because of any paranormal activity, but because it was falling apart.

The two of them held onto each other for a long while before Wendy placed Black back onto the floor.

"I really hope that mom wasn't brought in here into this." Wendy said, motioning towards the floor. "You're alright after that fall, but I don't think a person would be alright if they fell into that." Black couldn't have agreed more.

"Let's walk around, I saw a light on under the door over there." Black said and Wendy started to walk slowly around the hole. "Be careful because I don't know if the floor is weak in any other spots."

"I will." Wendy said and she stepped over a metal box that was sitting on the floor. She didn't know what it was, but she thought that it had been there for many years because of how dusty it was. When they had made it to the closed door, all of Wendy's nerves came back and fear hit her with full force. "We have to do this." She said more to herself than to Black. Black nodded his head and moved to the side of the door.

"Go on." Black said as he motioned for Wendy to open the door. Wendy took in a deep breath, but instead of hesitating like last time, she opened it slowly. The light in the room was purple like the rest of the house, but what she saw in the corner of the small room made her heart ache.

"Mom's purse!" she shouted and then out of the corner of her eye, she saw a white and slender figure stand up.

****

The figure in the corner of the room stood up when Wendy shouted and Wendy stopped dead in her tracks when she saw the figure move. What she saw was unlike anything that she had ever seen before. The figure was white from head to toe and it was oozing a white liquid as well. Wendy's breath caught in her throat when she saw the red eyes of the creature.

"Ahhh!" Wendy screamed at the top of her lungs and bent down quickly to grab Black.

"Wendy... wait!" Black shouted when she took off running. Wendy could hear the creature yelling something from behind her, but she didn't pay any attention to it.

"That was a ghost... a monster... whatever it was, it wasn't human!" Wendy screamed to Black as she made her way around the gaping hole in the floor.

"Wendy, there was something odd about what we just saw." Black said relatively calmly considering the graveness of their situation.

"I know! It was a monster!" Wendy screamed out irritably. There was no way that she could take on something like that. Wendy and Black needed to find a way outside of the haunted house so that they could call the police. "That thing is too much for us to handle Black. We have to call the police!" Wendy's lungs were beginning to burn from running for an extended period of time, but her legs kept moving.

"And tell them what Wendy?" Black said as he squirmed in Wendy's arms. She had a tight grip on Black and it was making it difficult for Black to breathe. "You can't tell them that you think that you saw a monster, they'll think you're crazy."

"I'll think of something." Wendy said as she somehow managed to find the front door. She placed Black down quickly onto the floor and tried to pry the door open. "It's no use. It's stuck on this side as well." Wendy said out of breath. She needed to get that door open and get out of the house as soon as possible. She regretted ever wanting to investigate that house in the first place. She should have listened to Black when he told her it would be a pointless case. Wendy was right about the place being haunted, but she wished that she hadn't had to find out this way.

"Wendy, I don't think that was a monster or a ghost. There was something odd about that thing that we saw." Wendy didn't have any time to argue with Black regarding the situation.

"Black," she said through gritted teeth. "I know what I saw and that was definitely not a human." Wendy said as her fingers trembled as she tried to get the wood off of the door. "It's no use, there has to be another exit." Just when she was about to go and kick out one of the boarded windows, Wendy heard a familiar voice.

"Wendy?" Wendy's head turned to the sound of the voice.

"Mom!"

CHAPTER FIVE

Wendy's cheeks reddened as her mother apologized profusely to Mr. Jackson and Black couldn't help but to laugh at Wendy's embarrassment. Apparently, Mr. Jackson bought the house so that he could fix it up because it was a hobby of his. He bought run down and fallen apart houses just so that he could make them brand new again.

"Stop laughing at me." Wendy mumbled under her breath to Black, but Black kept laughing.

"I'm sorry." Black said. If Black was able to cry, Wendy was confident that tears would be running down his furry cheeks. Apparently, Mr. Jackson was painting when Wendy's mother came over to the house with her gift bag from her and the neighbors. Startled by the loud banging on the door, Mr. Jackson had lost his footing on his ladder and a can of white paint had drenched him. His eyes were red from scrubbing the paint out of his eyes.

"No, you're not." Wendy said and pouted again. When her mother heard Mr. Jackson screaming in agony, she had come into the house through that back door and saw him lying on the floor. After she had sat him down in a chair, she had gone to the store to get Mr. Jackson some clothes.

"And what do you have to say to Mr. Jackson, young lady?" Mrs. Michaels walked over to Wendy and Black with her hands on her hips. Wendy lowered her eyes and told Mr. Jackson that she was sorry. Mrs. Michaels spent a long time scolding Wendy about breaking and entering into any house whether she thought it was abandoned or not.

Black was scolded as well, but he couldn't help but to keep laughing this time at himself instead of at Wendy. He finally realized that the reason why he couldn't sense anything in the house was because of the paint. Black didn't know why, but whenever paint was around, he couldn't sense anything anymore. His best guess at why this occurred was because of some odd effect from his paint allergy.

"My daughter will be here every weekend to help you fix up the place until you're done." This was part of Wendy's punishment and she winced. She knew that what she had done was wrong, but she thought that her mother's punishment was too brutal. Wendy went through all of this trouble to help her mother even though she wasn't in danger.

"I'm really sorry Mr. Jackson." Wendy said again as she walked out of the house through the back door.

"There's some more lightbulbs in the bag with the clothes." Mrs. Michaels said. Apparently the light in the rooms was purple because Mr. Jackson had grabbed the wrong bulbs from the store. As the three of them walked to Mrs. Michaels' car, Black stopped and looked back at the house and licked his paw clean.

"Come on Black." Wendy called out as she opened the car door for him. Black stared at the house for a few more moments. Black thought that their whole investigation had taken so many turns that he couldn't even predict what would happen next.

However, at the end of the day he was proud to say that he was right about the house not being haunted. Black was also happy to know that Wendy wouldn't be listening to rumors about anything without doing some investigating because one should never judge a book by its cover.

The End

CHARLIE
BOOK

Printed in Great Britain
by Amazon